What's Cooking, SpongeBob?

by James Gelsey

Illustrated by Clint Bond

SCHOLASTIC INC.

New York Toronto London Auckland Sydney
Mexico City New Delhi Hong Kong Buenos Aires

Stephen Hillenburg

Published by Scholastic Inc.,
90 Old Sherman Turnpike, Danbury, Connecticut 06816.

SCHOLASTIC and associated logos are trademarks
and/or registered trademarks of Scholastic Inc.

ISBN 0-439-56282-1

First Scholastic Printing, February 2004

Chapters

Mr. Krabs looked around his
restaurant, the Krusty Krab. It was
empty for the third day in a row.

FREE!

"Where's all me money—I mean, me customers?" Mr. Krabs asked.

"Probably watching Chef Kelp's new cooking show," replied Squidward Tentacles, who was watching TV to pass the time.

"Who in the name of Davy Jones's Locker is Chef Kelp?" asked Mr. Krabs.

"Chef Kelp is the Kitchen Magician," explained SpongeBob SquarePants, without taking his eyes off the screen. "He's my idol."

Mr. Krabs watched Chef Kelp toss a seaweed salad on television.

"Nutritious and delicious," Chef Kelp announced. "Not like those griddle-fried globs you get at restaurants."

"He's ruining me business!" Mr. Krabs cried. "This scallywag must be stopped!"

"What's a scallywag?" asked SpongeBob.

"Someone who wants to see me lose all me money," Mr. Krabs said.

"For more cooking magic, come to Chef Kelp's cooking school," came the announcer's voice as the show ended.

"That's it!" Mr. Krabs exclaimed. "SpongeBob, you're going to Chef Kelp's cooking school. We'll use his cooking secrets to make the Krusty Krab the most popular restaurant in all the Seven Seas!"

"And remember boy, not a word of our secret plan to anyone!" Mr. Krabs added.

"You can count on me, Mr. Krabs!" SpongeBob promised.

Back at home, SpongeBob told his best friend, Patrick Star, all about Mr. Krabs's secret plan.

"Yahoo!" Patrick cheered. "We're going to cooking school!"

"But it's supposed to be a secret, Patrick," SpongeBob said. "If you went, Mr. Krabs would know I told."

"No problem," Patrick said.

Patrick climbed up and buried himself
inside SpongeBob's head.

"Uh, Patrick," SpongeBob said. "You're . . .
a little . . . too heavy . . . for me."

Patrick jumped down. "I could pretend to be your spatula," he suggested.

SpongeBob shook his head. "No self-respecting chef would ever use a spatula that doesn't have the Good Pineapple-keeping Seal of Approval."

"I want to go to cooking school!" Patrick wailed. "I want to eat fancy foods with funny-sounding names!"

SpongeBob suddenly got an idea.

"That's it, Patrick!" SpongeBob said. "I'll pretend that I speak a foreign language. You can be my interpreter!"

But Patrick didn't understand.

"You'll turn my made-up language into real words," SpongeBob explained.

"Oh, like I do everyday," Patrick said.

"To cooking school we go!" SpongeBob declared.

On their way, SpongeBob and Patrick ran into their friend, Sandy Cheeks.

"Here's our chance to practice, Patrick," SpongeBob whispered. "Flork nub'n, Sandy, tie tuktin," SpongeBob said, waving.

Sandy stared at SpongeBob.

"SpongeBob, did you eat a bad Krabby Patty?" Sandy asked.

SpongeBob elbowed Patrick in the stomach.

"SpongeBob says you owe him five dollars," Patrick interpreted.

SpongeBob looked angrily at Patrick.

"Norgle splorgle blot blit!" he yelled.

"I mean, he says hi," said Patrick.

"SpongeBob, what has gotten into you?" Sandy asked.

"Just a little trick Patrick and I worked out for cooking school," SpongeBob explained.

"Why are you going to cooking school?" asked Sandy. "You're already the best fry cook I know."

SpongeBob started to explain. But then he remembered what Mr. Krabs had said.

"Sorry, Sandy," SpongeBob said. "But there's a little voice in my head that won't let me tell you."

Patrick poked his head out from inside SpongeBob's head. "That voice was me, SpongeBob," Patrick said. "I came back for the candy bar I left in here before."

SpongeBob and Patrick waited outside
Chef Kelp's kitchen.

"I'm really nervous about meeting Chef

Chef Kelp

Kelp," SpongeBob said. "Do you have any words of advice, Patrick?"

"Oooh, look at me," Patrick said. He danced around the room, singing, "I'm a giant popover! I'm a giant popover!"

SpongeBob finally gathered his courage
and went into the kitchen.

"A new student," Chef Kelp said.
"What is your name?"

SpongeBob tried to answer,
but no words came out. He
was too nervous.

"Uh . . . I . . . um . . . ," he stammered.

"I don't understand," Chef Kelp said.

"I . . . er . . . blinkle wag sniffel tun!" SpongeBob blurted out.

Through the door, Patrick heard
SpongeBob's funny words and sprang
into action. "I can translate!
I can translate!"
Patrick shouted.

"I'm coming, SpongeBob!" Patrick threw open the kitchen door, smashing into Chef Kelp.

"SpongeBob says that you're his cooking idol," Patrick translated. "And that you should give me some chocolate."

Patrick looked around but didn't see Chef Kelp anywhere.

"Where'd he go?" asked Patrick.

SpongeBob pointed to the floor.

"Funny place to take a nap," Patrick said.

"He's not taking a nap! Chef Kelp's out cold!" SpongeBob whispered frantically. "Do you know what this means, Patrick?"

"He's not going to give me any chocolate?" Patrick asked sadly.

"It means that Mr. Krabs's plan is ruined," SpongeBob said. "How can I learn Chef Kelp's secrets if he's senseless, KO'd, dead to the world, in the land of Nod?"

"Maybe you should put on his magicky hat," Patrick suggested.

"Do I dare put on Chef Kelp's official Kitchen Magician hat?" SpongeBob wondered. He tried to imagine what would happen if he did.

"I'll do it!" SpongeBob said. He put on Chef
Kelp's hat and apron. "You know, Patrick, I'm
starting to feel cheflike already," he said.

"That's good," Patrick said. "'Cause the students are coming in for the cooking class."

Chapter 5
Someone's in the Kitchen with SpongeBob

When the other cooking students arrived, they all looked at SpongeBob expectantly.

"We're ready to begin, Chef Kelp," one finally said.

SpongeBob spun around. "Chef Kelp?" SpongeBob repeated. "He's *here?*"

One of the students pointed at SpongeBob. "Aren't you Chef Kelp?" she asked. "I mean, you're wearing the Kitchen Magician hat and all."

"Yeah . . . um . . . that's me, Chef Kelp,"
SpongeBob sputtered. "I'm certainly not
some lowly fry cook just wearing his hat
and apron."

"So how about some of that kitchen
magic of yours, Chef?"
asked another of
the students.

All of the students cheered.

"Let's give it a try," SpongeBob said,
shrugging.

SpongeBob

began waving his spatula

like he was conducting an

orchestra. The students started

cooking like crazy.

"We're slicing, tossing, mincing, saucing,"

sang SpongeBob. "Grating and beating and dicing—"

"—and eating!" Patrick chimed in.

"And chopping and seeding, but be careful, no bleeding!" SpongeBob added.

"Hooray for Chef Kelp!" the students cheered.

"Now what are you going to prepare with all of this?" one student asked.

SpongeBob suddenly panicked. He didn't know what to make!

Chapter 6
Cooking with
SpongeBob ChefPants

SpongeBob wondered what he could cook that would impress his students.

"I've got it!" SpongeBob announced. "Step aside, everyone."

SpongeBob set to work, moving like lightning across the kitchen.

He opened every cabinet, used every pan, left no spice unturned.

Finally, he was finished. SpongeBob smiled and held out a plate. "I give you— the Krabby Patty!" he announced.

A soft *Ooooooooooo* filled the kitchen. The
cooking students gazed in awe at the patty
and studied it intently.

SpongeBob smiled at the applauding
students.

"I think my work here is done," he said.

"Mine, too," Patrick said, pointing to the
pile of empty bowls and plates.

"Let's go home, Patrick," SpongeBob said.

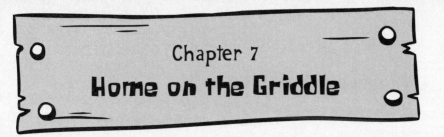

Chapter 7
Home on the Griddle

SpongeBob and Patrick returned to the Krusty Krab.

"SpongeBob, me boy!" Mr. Krabs said. "What kind of secrets did you steal, I mean, learn?"

"Well, Mr. Krabs, I didn't exactly get to—" SpongeBob began to say.

"Mr. Krabs! Look at this!" Squidward suddenly shouted.

Chef Kelp's face filled the television screen.

" . . . and when I woke up, I discovered the most delicious food ever," he announced. He raised the plate SpongeBob had left behind. On it sat a Krabby Patty.

"It's a Krabby Patty!" Patrick exclaimed.

Mr. Krabs's eyes lit up.

"Now everyone run out and get yourselves one of these griddle-fried globs of magic!" Chef Kelp told his television audience.

Instantly the doors to the Krusty Krab flew open. Crowds of customers poured inside.

Mr. Krabs rushed over to SpongeBob. "You saved the Krusty Krab, SpongeBob!" he cried, with tears of joy in his eyes. "Now go into the kitchen and work some of that magic of yours!"

SpongeBob went into the kitchen. "Chef
Kelp can keep his magic hat," he said. "Just
give me a griddle, a Krabby Patty, and a
spatula to flip it."

"Snorgle, gorgle, flub dub!" Patrick called
from the kitchen door.

SpongeBob smiled. "I couldn't have said
it better myself, Patrick!"